TONGUE TWISTERS FOR TERRIBLE PEOPLE

TONGUE TWISTERS

for terrible people

Bud rOSE

Tongue Twisters for Terrible People

Published by Bound/Unbound
An imprint of Exsolutas Press

ISBN: 978-1-7364642-3-6

Cover, book design and illustrations by Coverkitchen.

This book is dedicated to the memories of all those who gave their lives for gender and sexual self-expression rights.

WARNING: CONTENTS ARE HOT!

Do **not** read if:

You can't read the letters BDSM without wincing.

You are 100% asexual.

You've never had a kinky fantasy and never want one.

You are under 18 years old without parental permission.

You hate tongue twisters.

Nothing excites you. Ever.

You believe sex should never be the *butt* of humor.

Contents

O, Orifice

O Orifice, o Orifice, do you prefer the plug or fist?
Plunging penis, preferably? Or dildo
twisted from the wrist?
O Orifice, o Orifice, how many holes in one?
Penis, dildo, fist and plug plumb each of you in frantic fun.

Sue-Sue's Sheers

Sue-Sue sashayed in sheers so high
His nipples nipped their waist.
He shook his shoulders shimmying,
Though to twerk was more his taste.

Poopy-Cake

Miss Mary Mack, Mack, Mack
All dressed in black, black, black,
With sharpened spikes, spikes, spikes,
All down her back, back, back.

She asked her lover, lover, lover
With fifty begs, begs, begs,
To watch his lover, lover, lover
Fucked with two pegs, pegs, pegs.

They fucked her long, long, long,
Starred in a song, song, song,
Mack never went back, back, back
To craving shlong, shlong, shlong.

Zelda and Xander

Zelda's zinger zings Xander's zapper.
Xander zaps Zelda's zinger.
Zingers, zappers; zappers, zingers:
Zelda and Xander, zoological swingers.

Teddied and Tassled

Teddied-Toni tooted Tassled-Teddi's titties.
Tasseled-Teddi tweaked Teddied-Toni's tushie.
Tasseled-Teddi tongued Teddied-Toni's tonsils.
Teddied-Toni tasted Tassled-Teddi's tootsies.

Maso's Needs

Gagged and tied and swung from beams,
Grabs and tugs sate Maso's needs.
Whipped and wrapped and open slapped,
"Wayward! Warped! You wicked chap!"
In gutter-sludge and Marla's fudge,
Maso's heart's engorged with love.

Kama Sutra Instructions

Ken and Karly come to kink
By way of Kama Sutra ink:
Lift Karly's leg up Kenny's chest;
On Karly's thigh, Ken's buttocks rest,
With Karly's mouth, suck Kenny up,
Thrust Kenny's thumb up Karly's butt,
Throb and pump and slip and slide.
Cum and repeat: the other side.

Alpha Bella

Blind Betty beseeched Ben to bite her butterfly,
But Bella bit Blind Betty's butterfly first.
Biding his time, Ben bit Betty's butterfly
Upon Alpha Bella's butterfly-abated thirst.

When You Can't Ski

Waiting out the winds at Wyndham,
Wendy went for Willie's dick some.
Whisking off Wendy's gaters,
From below her, Willie ate her.

Bending Wendy down the front,
Willie bared her bouncing butt.
Wendy, bolted on his woody head,
Bashed butt to balls until both bled.

Sweating out the winds at Windham,
Willie and Wendy licked their lips some.
Wagged and wasted, they wiggled in some
Skiing pants while wet with whizzum.

Spoons and Forks

Saul spooned Paul and
Paul spooned Saul.
Shelly, who hated spooning,
Forked Saul while forking Paul.

Dacha Orgy

On Duscha's verge, young Vera squats,
Their vulvae flood with gluey hots.
Svetlana's clit's in Vera's mouth,
Svetlana shakes from navel south.
In Vera, Yuri's popping prick hops
Up and down — a pogo stick.
Svetlana's sweaty ass and hips
Are sucked right raw by Anna's lips,
While Duscha's dildo plunges deep
In Anna's anus 'til she weeps.

Shawn's Beast

Who saw Esau swing Shawn's beast?
Shawn saw Esau swing Shawn's beast.
Esau saw Shawn see him swing,
So Shawn said, "Esau, suck this thing."

Post-Op Partsies

Vinnie's vaggie's very new.
Vinnie's vain: waves vag on view.
Vickers vies for new-vag-Vin,
Post-op-peenie pulsates in.

Popular Proper Perry Pandy

How many poopers did Perry Pandy plug?
How many pluggeds did Perry Pandy love?
How many peenies plugged Perry Pandy proper?
How many Perry-pluggeds were Perry Pandy toppers?

Moist

Sal's saliva soaked Val's vagina.
Val's vagina sopped Sal's saliva.
Sal and Val Frenched tongue in clit,
Lips and petals suction-zipped.

Doo-be-do-be-doo

If Dickie's dick dug Daryl's dooer,
Daryl's dick dug Peter's pooer,
And Dino's dick dug Sheldon's shitter:
Would Sheldon's shlong and Peter's prick
Pump Dickie's, Daryl's or Dino's dumper?

Chachi's Cheeks

Chachi's cheeks are red and sore
From Willa's whip; he groans for more.
Chachi's balls are bound and bulging.
Patty prods them while indulging.
Chachi's eyes are shut up tight
His mouth stuffed full of Mica's might.

What's that in her Shoes with Lifts?

Sure, she wished she'd shed her shift,
Pulled panties past her shoes with lifts,
Pulled, right down, proud Petra's pants
Then drove her dildo while they danced.

(Not for nothing, naked dances are
Sequestered, private prances.
Dips and bobs and salsa moves
To finger fucks and tonguing grooves.)

Petra played Miss Prim, Miss Priss,
Then showered her with golden piss.
How she wished she'd shed her shift,
Pulled panties past her shoes with lifts.

Gallery of Gaggy Giggles

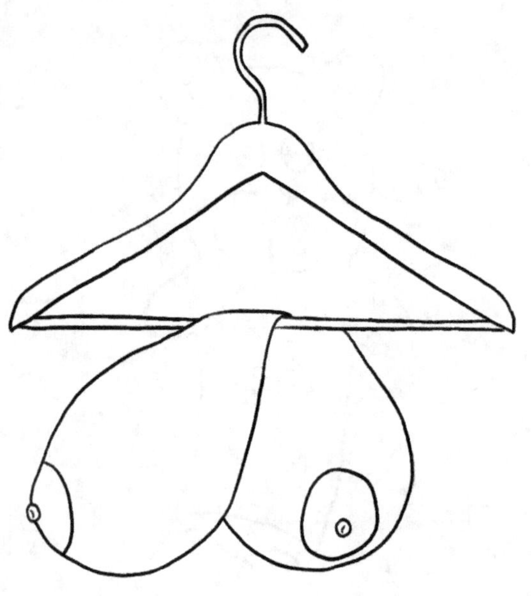

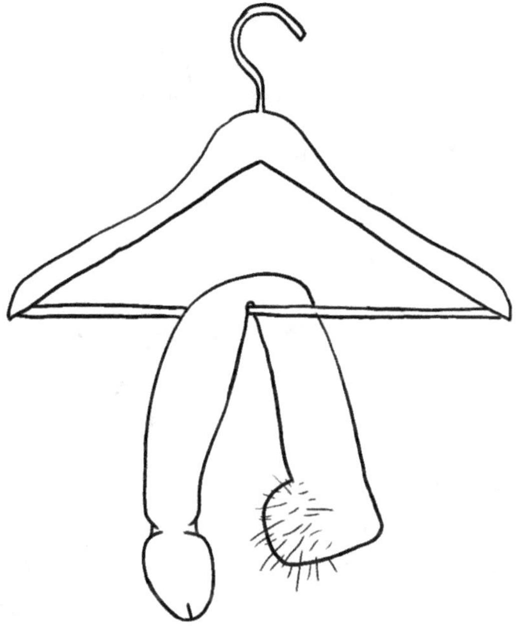

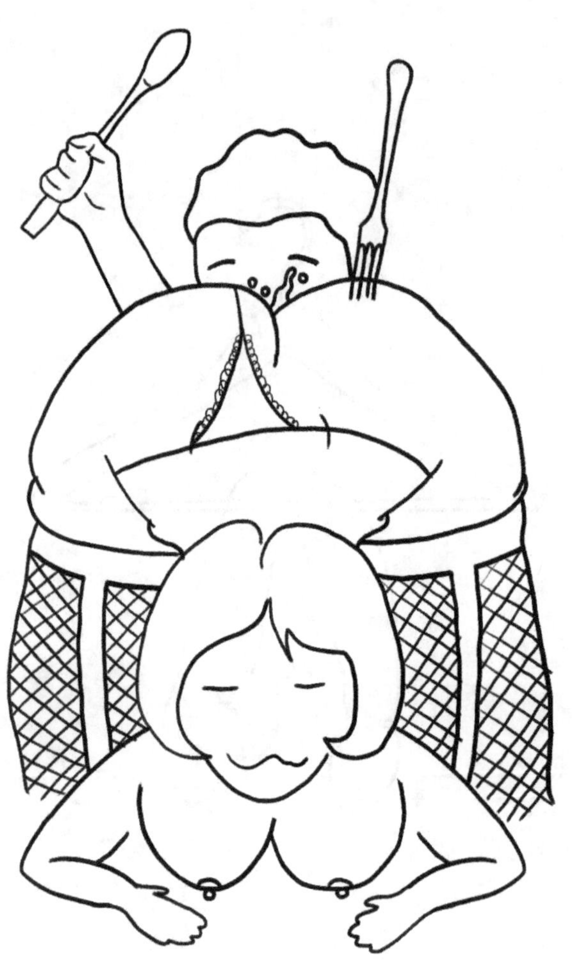

Gallery of Gaggy Giggles

While wicked words
Work their wonky way through,
Punky pictures pique from
Playful pages-full.

Drawings drip with
Daft dispropriety,
Easing newly freakish
Sex anxiety.

Color ours in
Red and fleshy crayons;
Draw your mind's eye pix of
Kink-toons you crave on.

Poly Polly

If poly Polly plied Peter and Paulie
And Peter plied Paula
And Paulie plied Penny,
And Penny plied Pattie,
While Pattie and Paula plied Polly,
How many polies did poly Polly ply?

Conjoined

Conjoined Connie craves cunnilingus.
Conjoined Carrie craves rimming too.
Connie and Carrie rim cunnilingus,
With conjoined cunts and twice the poo.

Randy and Raye of Reading

Randy Randy rode 'round Reading,
Waving his raging woodie.
Randy Raye, ready and sweaty,
Ran and leapt on Randy's woodie.
Reddening residents, rapt at
Raye's and Randy's riding rutting,
Ran rampant, rutting all 'round Reading.

Peter's Pecker

Peter's pecker pecked a pack of pudgy Peggies.
How many pudgy Peggies did Peter's pecker peck?

Dang those Danglers!

Daily, Dilly dallied with his dildo deeply dangled.
Dolly dared to dilly-dally with her dildo dangled.
Dilly's dildo dangled. Dolly's dildo dangled.
Dang Dilly's and Dolly's dangling dildoes!

Omar and Mario in Lust

Omar ooohs when Mario oozes.
Mario ooohs when Omar oozes.
Both oozers oooh at dirty movies,
Both ooohers ooze at dirty movies.
Omar obliquely obliges Mario's oozing,
Mario moves on Omar's oozing,
Deaf to movie-goers' dirty ooohing.

No Blueberries Here!

Billie bent to blow blueberries up Bertie's butt.
Beet-red Bertie batted Billie's blueberries away.
Billie begged, but Bertie said, "No blueberries up my butt!"
Sad Billie bagged the blueberries, then bagged
Bertie 'til they both had blue ballies.

Sex Sandwiches on the Sofa

Sally and Cissy sell sex sandwiches on the sofa.
Saul submits to a sex sandwich on the sofa.
Sally sucks Cissy's clit's slit sauce.
Saul stubs his stump down Sally's slit.
Cissy slides sham-shlong up Saul's shit shaft.
Saul slurps savory Sally's sub-slit shit.

Formerly Known As

Leslie nee Lester
Lusts for Sammy nee Sally.
Sammy nee Sally
Salivates for Bobbie nee Bobby.
Bobbie nee Bobby
Begs for Jeannie nee Jimmy.
Jeannie nee Jimmy
Joneses for Evan nee Ellen.
Evan nee Ellen
Enlists Leslie nee Lester, though
Leslie nee Lester
Lusts for Sammy nee Sally.

Aphrodite's Appetitee

Alabaster Aphrodite added up her appetitee:
Alexander and 'Ermione, all day long and into nightee.
Alexander and 'Ermione sated Aphrodite's appetitee:
All day long and into nightee, felatio and cunnilayngee.

Bad, Bad Larry

Latex Lucy laced up Larry
Lashed him up like cash and carry,
Lit him up by licking loosely,
Lost a glass plug up his hoosie,
Lanced him with stilletto heels,
And seared hot wax with sterling seals.

Domestic Bliss

When Brutish Barb bent o'er her duster,
Barb's Bud bounced his cock erect.
Bud waved his flagpole at high muster.
Barb polished it between her breasts.

Dreams of Drake

Dino's dildo dug down Dara,
Dara dreamt the dildo's Drake.
Drake dug Dino dildoing Dara,
Dino dug Dara's dreams of Drake.

Wee Willie's Wee Willie

Willie worried his willy was too wee.
Wanda wouldn't waste words on Willie,
Whose willy really was too wee.

Cocks of Steel

Rick and Dick crave cocks and rocks
Dick and Rick crave real and steel.
Rick's rocks are real rocks.
Dick's cocks are steel cocks.
Dick docks Rick's rocks.
Rick rocks Dick's cocks.
Rick feels steel cocks.
Dick feels real rocks.
Dick steels Rick's rocks.
Rick rocks Dick's steel.
Dick's cocks are rocked while
Rick's rocks are steel-cocked.

Frocks and Cocks

Keith Kearney kicks his cock up Frank Field's frock.
Frank Field face fucks Keith Kearney's cock.
Keith Kearney favors the forceful thrust
While Frank Field craves a cockful suck.

Ramona La Rue

Ramona La Rue sucked cunt and cock, too.
Laid Lesbian lads and popped penis in poo.
Ramona, he rode a girl goat to ground,
Got fucked by a bison and made not a sound.

Freddie Frister the Famous Fister

Freddie Frister, the famous fister
Fists for free and fists for fun.
Fists plunged up in frickin' fashion,
Fists for cash and on the run.
Fists so fast you frickin' can't win,
Fists far up esophagus.
Fists in front with girls while kissing
Fists up butts of men in luck.
Freddie Frister, the famous fister,
Fists in flight and fists to fuck.

Take Yer Turn

Whatcha waitin' for, more silly songs?
Take yer terse turn twisting tongues!

Wee Willy Winkie can wun through town;
You can write wet weirdness down.

Sue's staid seashells sold at shore;
Your freakish fun shall sell for more!

Bud Rose is the nom de ticklish plume of an American poet, translator and philanthropist. Bud believes that the only moral issue regarding sex is consent among those who are fully free to withhold consent. An un-queer, un-freakish love life is but one choice among many fulfilling configurations.

www.ingramcontent.com/pod-product-compliance
Lightning Source LLC
Chambersburg PA
CBHW061223210726
48294CB00006B/1961
9781736464212